EXERC

RAYMOND QUENEAU

Translated by Barbara Wright

A NEW DIRECTIONS BOOK

First published in France as *Exercises de Style* in 1947
   by Editions Gallimard.
The music on page 124 is by Pierre Philippe and is in his handwriting.
Initials and permutations of the author's photograph are
   by Stefan Themerson.

First published as New Directions Paperbook 513 in 1981
Published simultaneously in Canada by George J. McLeod Ltd.,
   Toronto.

Library of Congress Cataloging in Publication Data

Queneau, Raymond, 1903-1976.
   Exercises in style.

   Translation of 1st ed. (1947) of Exercises de style.
   I. Title.
PQ2633.U43E93   1981   848'.91207   80-26102
ISBN 0-8112-0789-7 (pbk.)

New Directions Books are published for James Laughlin
by New Directions Publishing Corporation
80 Eighth Avenue, New York 10011

SECOND PRINTING

1231
2312
3123

see : permutations, pages 129-133

CONTENTS

NOTES FOR THE 1981 AMERICAN
PAPERBACK EDITION

Asked whether, to herald this new edition of the *Exercises in Style,* I might have anything to add to my 1958 preface, I was a little surprised to discover that I did indeed have quite a bit to add. By now the book is very well known in many countries and has maybe even become a classic, but literati the whole world over still have a great deal to learn from the simple, mocking, amused linguistic lesson that Queneau here conceals beneath his characteristic humor. Prophets proverbially getting more of a raw deal in their own countries than elsewhere, it is perhaps the French who have learned the least. To take a few categories at random: would anyone like to assert that French art critics, sociologists, or philosophers, have been converted to Queneau's thesis that it is rather a good idea to write a) unpretentiously, and b) so that we, the vulgar, can understand them?

Since 1947 there have been at least six new editions of this book in France, one of them a superb luxury affair, with each variation printed in a different typographical form invented by Massin, and the whole followed by "33 parallel exercises in style, drawn, painted and sculpted by Carelman." In the introduction to that (1963) edition, Queneau explains that the idea for the *Exercises* came to him in the 1930s, after he and his friend Michel Leiris had attended a concert at the Salle Pleyel where Bach's *The Art of Fugue* had been played. What particularly struck Queneau about this piece was that, although based on a rather slight theme, its variations "proliferated almost to infinity." It would be interesting, he thought, to create a similar work of literature.

By 1942 he had produced the first 12 variations on his "slight theme." These were refused by the puzzled editor of "an extremely distinguished literary review." Undismayed, Queneau kept adding exercises over the years until by 1946 he had composed 99. "I stopped there," he wrote, "judging this quantity to be sufficient; neither too many nor too few: the Greek ideal, you might say." All the later published editions stop at 99 too, though in the most recent (unornamented) edition (1973) there are some no doubt significant expulsions and substitutions, which I'll say more about later. In spite of this self-imposed restriction to 99 for the purposes of the ideal Greek volume, Queneau later published further exercises in various reviews, and in the luxury volume I have mentioned he gives us in an appendix a list of "possible exercises in style"—no less than 124 of them!—ranging from "The Seven Deadly Sins" to a further plethora of abstruse rhetorical terms such as anacoluthon, or anadiplosis. (The conscientious reader of the present volume may well consider, however, that he has already enlarged his rhetorical vocabulary quite sufficiently. Translating it did wonders for mine.)

The translation is based on the original 1947 French publication, and nothing has been changed from the first English edition. I was given the opportunity to make the odd discreet revision, but I decided that rather than mess about with a word here or there I would prefer to let the whole stand as it is. There are certainly a few words that I would write differently today, but I don't think they stand out too flagrantly. On a rereading, I was at first a little taken aback by, for instance, the expression "teddy boy," but I was quite reassured when I found it in your very own most recent Webster, where it is defined as : "A young British hoodlum who affects Edwardian dress." Maybe the study of what would automatically have been translated differently in 1981 would be an amusing exercise in style in itself.

A few remarks about some of the substitutions (approved by Queneau) in my version. It wouldn't have made any sense to try to reproduce *in English* the way French peasants (in the nineteenth century) spoke French. There wouldn't have been any point, either, in informing Anglo-Saxons about the way Italians tend to pronounce French. In the former case I substituted *West Indian,* and I had the greatest fun in lifting phrases and expressions wholesale from Samuel Selvon's marvelous book *The Lonely Londoners.* In substituting *Opera English* for *Italianismes* I had just as much fun, and it was also in a mild sort of way an act of revenge. I had translated three classical operas. With some reluctance, I might add, because, without *too* much exaggeration, it seemed to me that just about the whole of the libretti consisted in the protagonists declaiming—at great length—either: "Ah, how I suffer!," or: "Ah! I am in raptures!" However, I did them, and apart from superhuman efforts to make the texts singable, I also tried to make them as simple and as little ecstatic as possible. But this made some of the singers a little uneasy. Unless the phrases were of the order of: "Ah! if to do it he continues . . . .," they had the vague feeling that they weren't really poetic. I understood how this had come about when I studied some of the published—and much sung—opera translations of the time. So in *Opera English* I took great—and perhaps sneaky—satisfaction in appropriating whole phrases from these well-worn translations. To take just one example, I swear to you that "His words deep within my heart are sculptured" is stolen, *in toto,* from one of these poetic libretti.

A confession about the *Modern Style* exercise. In 1958, way before the recent revival of "art nouveau," I simply didn't know the strange fact that for this particular *genre* the French use English words—which are translated into English by French words. I refuse to take the entire responsibility for the discrepancy in style here, though, because I consulted Queneau and naively asked him what sort of English "modern style" he thought I should use. He replied that he wasn't qualified to advise me. With hindsight, I now tend to think that he was thus amusing himself hugely at my ignorance. However that may be, I solved (?) the problem by once again having fun, and shoving in all the (modern) journalistic clichés I could think of.

And now a word about Queneau's own substitutions in his 1973 edition. *Reactionary* and *Feminine,* for example, have been expunged, and replaced respectively, and perhaps mysteriously, by *Ensembliste* (which I think has something to do with "set theory"), and *Lipogramme.* A lipogram, as of course you know (although your abovementioned Webster won't help you if you don't), is "a writing from which all words are omitted which contain a particular letter." Here, Queneau has performed the staggering feat of writing a whole exercise without using the letter E—the most boringly characterless of all letters, because the most common. For *Haiku* he has substituted *Tanka:* "An unrhymed Japanese verse form of five lines containing 5,7,5,7, and 7 syllables respectively—compare HAIKU." In his *Haiku,* Queneau, with his oh so justifiable poetic license, omitted one of the obligatory classical elements—the reference to one of the four seasons. (Naturally, I, in my pedantic way, restored it: "Summer S. . . .") Just in case you might feel cheated not to have his *Tanka,* I'll translate it for you here, for free:

> The S bus arrives
> A behatted dude gets in
> There follows a clash
> Later outside Saint-Lazare
> There is talk of a button

There's still a whole lot more I'd love to have room to say. Such as that, whereas in my 1958 preface I amateurishly analyzed Queneau's exercises into "roughly 7 different groups," the sumptuous 1963 illustrated edition includes, as a bonus, a real, proper, professional analysis by Dr. Claude Leroy, a psychiatrist, who compares Queneau's "deformation of language" with that obsessionally practised by some psychiatric patients, for reasons best known to their unconscious. This essay is called: "Study on the loss of information and the variation in meaning in Raymond Queneau's *Exercises in Style.*" And though the doctor ends his study by describing it as "long and weighty, and, like all analyses, destructive. . . ." it is actually of the greatest fascination, and one more pointer to the fact that, however funny we may find Queneau's exercises—and even after all this time, many of them still make even me laugh aloud—there is a great deal more to them than funniness.

Which brings me back to my original preface. Just

two remarks. Firstly: *Le Chiendent,* which I there called "one of the easiest to read of all Queneau's novels," was translated some years ago under the title *The Bark Tree* and, so far as I know, is still available. And lastly: The Paris metro no longer smells of garlic. It is the cleanest, best, and most efficient system of public transport in the whole of my limited experience of the public transport systems of the world.

BARBARA WRIGHT

PREFACE

Ladies and Gentlemen:[*]
From time to time people politely ask me what I am translating now.

So I say: a book by Raymond Queneau.

They usually react to that in one of 3 different ways.

Either they say: that must be difficult.

Or they say: Who's he?

Or they say: Ah.

Of those three reactions, let's take the third—as the fortune-tellers say.

People say: Ah.

By: Ah—they don't mean quite the same as the people who say: Who's he? They mean that they don't know who Queneau is, but that don't much care whether they know or not. However, since, as I said, this sort of conversation is usually polite, they often go on to enquire: What book of his are you translating?

So I say: *Exercices de Style,*

And then, all over again, they say: Ah.

At this point I usually feel it would be a good idea

[*] Based on a talk given in the Gaberbocchus Common Room on April 1st 1958.

to say something about this book, *Exercices de Style*, but as it's rather difficult to know where to begin, if I'm not careful I find that my would-be explanation goes rather like this:

"Oh yes, *you* know, it's the story of a chap who gets into a bus and starts a row with another chap who he thinks keeps treading on his toes on purpose, and Queneau repeats the same story 99 times in a different ways—it's terribly good . . . "

So I've come to the conclusion that it is thus my own fault when these people I have been talking about finally stop saying "Ah" and tell me that it's a pity I always do such odd things. It's not that my wooffly description is inaccurate—there are in fact 99 exercises, they all do tell the same story about a minor brawl in a bus, and they are all written in a different style. But to say that much doesn't explain anything, and the *Exercices* and the idea behind them probably do need some explanation.

In essaying an explanation, or rather, perhaps, a proper description, I have an ally in this gramophone record, which has recently been made in France, of 22 of the 99 *exercices*. It is declaimed and sung by *les Frères Jacques*—who have been likened to the English Goons. You will hear that the record is very funny. I said it was an ally, yet on the other hand it may be an enemy, because it may lead you to think that the *exercices* are just funny and nothing else. I should like to return to this point later, but first I want to say something about the author of the *Exercices*.

Raymond Queneau has written all the books you see here on the table—and others which I haven't been able to get hold of. He is a poet—not just a writer of poetry, but a poet in the wider sense. He is also a scholar and mathematician. He is a member of the

10

Académie Goncourt (and they have only 10 members, in comparison with the 40 of the Académie Française), and he is one of the top boys of the publishing house of Gallimard. But he is a kind of writer who tends to puzzle people in this country because of his breadth and range—you can't classify him. He is one of the most influential and esteemed people in French literature—but he can write a poem like this:

> Ce soir
> si j'écrivais un poème
> pour la postérité?
>
> fichtre
> la belle idée
>
> je me sens sûr de moi
> j'y vas
> et
>
> à
> la
> postérité
> j'y dis merde et remerde
> et reremerde
>
> drôlement feintée
> la postérité
> qui attendait son poème
>
> ah mais

Queneau, you see, is not limited, and he doesn't take himself over-seriously. He's too wise. He doesn't limit himself to being either serious or frivolous—or even, I might say, to being either a scientist or an artist. He's both. He uses everything that he finds in life for his poetry—and even things that he doesn't find in life, such as a mathematically disappearing dog, or a proud trojan horse who sits in a French bar and drinks gin fizzes with silly humans.* And all this is, I think, the reason why you find people in England who don't know who Queneau is. Two of his novels were published here, by John Lehmann, in English translations, about 10 years ago. They were, I think, not very successful here. Even though the critics thought they were writing favourably about them. I was looking through the reviews of one of them—*Pierrot*—the other day, and this brings me back to what I was saying about Queneau's wit and lightness of touch being possibly misleading—the book's very brilliance seemed to blind the critics to the fact that it was *about* anything. The *New Statesman* wrote: "*Pierrot* is *simply* a light-hearted little fantasy . . .", and *Time & Tide* came down to Parish Magazine style: "This novel is of the kind called 'so very french'. It is all very unassuming and amusing, and most of us enjoy this kind of fun." According to the current way of thinking (or not-thinking), it seems that if we are to enjoy anything then we must not have to think about it, and, conversely, if we are to think about anything, then we mustn't enjoy it. This is a calamitous and idiotic division of functions.

And this, I think, brings me to the *Exercices de Style*. Queneau is a linguist, and he also has a passionate interest in the French language. He has given a lot of thought to one aspect of it—the French language as *actually spoken*. *In Bâtons, Chiffres et Lettres*, he

* *The Trojan Horse & At the Edge of the Forest.* Gaberbocchus

12

writes: "I consider spoken French to be a different language, a very different language, from written French." And in the same book, he says: "I came to realise that modern written French must free itself from the conventions which still hem it in, (conventions of style, spelling and vocabulary) and then it will soar like a butterfly away from the silk cocoon spun by the grammarians of the 16th century and the poets of the 17th century. It also seemed to me that the first statement of this new language should be made not by describing some popular event in a novel (because people could mistake one's intentions), but, in the same way as the men of the 16th century used the modern languages instead of latin for writing their theological or philosophical treatises, to put some philosophical dissertation into spoken French."

Queneau did in fact "put some philosophical dissertation into spoken French"—Descartes' *Discours de la Méthode*. At least, he says that it was with this idea in mind that he started to write "something which later became a novel called *le Chiendent*." I won't say anything about the correspondence between it and *le Chiendent* now, but this novel, *le Chiendent*, is one of the easiest to read of all Queneau's novels, and also one of the most touching and thought-provoking. It is also almost farcically funny in parts.

This research into language is, of course, carried on in the *Exercices*. You get plenty of variations of the way different people actually speak—casual, noble, slang, feminine, etc. But you may have noticed that the exercise on p.129 starts like this:

JO UN VE UR MI RS SU DI AP RL TE
(that's in French, by the way. The English translation naturally looks quite different:

ED ON TO AY RD WA ID SM YO DA HE

13

Now please don't think that I'm going to try to persuade you that this is Queneau's idea of how anyone speaks French. You can't really discover 99 different ways of speaking one language. Well, perhaps you can, but you don't find them in the *Exercices*. I have analysed the 99 variations into roughly 7 different groups. The first—different types of speech. Next, different types of written prose. These include the style of a publisher's blurb, of an official letter, the "philosophic" style, and so on. Then there are 5 different poetry styles, and 8 exercises which are character sketches through language—reactionary, biased, abusive, etc. Fifthly there is a large group which experiments with different grammatical and rhetorical forms; sixthly, those which come more or less under the heading of *jargon*, and lastly, all sorts of odds and ends whose classification I'm still arguing about. This group includes the one quoted above, which is called: *permutations by groups of 2, 3, 4 and 5 letters*. Under *jargon* you get, for instance, one variation which tells the story in mathematical terms, one using as many botanical terms as possible, one using greek roots to make new words, and one in dog latin.

All this could be so clever that it could be quite ghastly and perfectly unreadable. But in fact I saw somewhere that *Exercices de Style* is Queneau's best seller among the French public. I have already intimated that however serious his purpose, Queneau is much more likely to write a farce than a pedantic treatise. His purpose here, in the *Exercices*, is, I think, a profound exploration into the possibilities of language. It is an experiment in the philosophy of language. He pushes language around in a multiplicity of directions to see what will happen. As he is a virtuoso of language and likes to amuse himself and

14

his readers, he pushes it a bit further than might appear necessary—he exaggerates the various styles into a reductio ad absurdum—ad lib., ad inf., and sometimes. —the final joke—ad nauseam.

I am saying a lot about what *I* think, but Queneau himself has had something to say about it. In a published conversation with Georges Ribemont-Dessaignes, he says: "In *les Exercices de Style*, I started from a real incident, and in the first place I told it 12 times in different ways. Then a year later I did another 12, and finally there were 99. People have tried to see it as an attempt to demolish literature—that was not at all my intention. In any case my intention was merely to produce some exercises; the finished product may possibly act as a kind of rust-remover to literature, help to rid it of some of its scabs. If I have been able to contribute a little to this, then I am very proud, especially if I have done it without boring the reader too much."

That Queneau *has* done this without boring the reader *at all*, is perhaps the most amazing thing about his book. Imagine how boring it might have been— 99 times the same story, and a story which has no point, anyway! I have spent more than a year, off and on, on the English version of the *Exercices*, but I haven't yet found any boredom attached to it. The more I go into each variation, the more I see in it. And the point about the original story having *no* point, is one of *the* points of the book. So much knowledge and comment on life is put into this pointless story. It's also important that it should be the same story all the time. Anybody can—and automatically does—describe different things in different ways. You don't speak poetically to the man in the ticket office at Victoria when you want to ask him for "two third returns, Brighton." Nor, as Jesperson points out, do you say to him : "Would you please sell me two third-class tickets from London to Brighton and back again, and I will pay you the usual fare for such tickets." Queneau's tour-de-force lies in the fact that the simplicity and banality of the material he starts from gives birth to so much.

This brings me to the last thing I want to say, which is about the English version. Queneau told me that the *Exercices* was one of his books which he would like to be translated—(he didn't suggest by whom). At the time I thought he was crazy. I thought that the book was an experiment with the French language as such, and therefore as untranslatable as the smell of garlic in the Paris metro. But I was wrong. In the same way as the story *as such* doesn't matter, the particular language it is written in doesn't matter as such. Perhaps the book is an exercise in communication patterns, whatever their linguistic sounds. And it seems to me that Queneau's attitude of enquiry and examination can, and perhaps should?—be applied to every language, and that is what I have tried to achieve with the English version.

B. W.

EXERCISES IN STYLE

otation

In the S bus, in the rush hour. A chap of about 26, felt hat with a cord instead of a ribbon, neck too long, as if someone's been having a tug-of-war with it. People getting off. The chap in question gets annoyed with one of the men standing next to him. He accuses him of jostling him every time anyone goes past. A snivelling tone which is meant to be aggressive. When he sees a vacant seat he throws himself on to it.

Two hours later, I meet him in the Cour de Rome, in front of the gare Saint-Lazare. He's with a friend who's saying: "You ought to get

an extra button put on your overcoat." He
shows him where (at the lapels) and why.

Double Entry

Towards the middle of the day and at midday I happened to be on and got on to the platform and the balcony at the back of an S-line and of a Contrescarpe-Champerret bus and passenger transport vehicle which was packed and to all intents and purposes full. I saw and noticed a young man and an old adolescent who was rather ridiculous and pretty grotesque; thin neck and skinny windpipe, string and cord round his hat and tile. After a scrimmage and scuffle he says and states in a lachrymose and snivelling voice and tone that his neighbour and fellow-traveller is deliberately trying and doing his utmost to push him and obtrude himself on him every time anyone gets off and makes an exit. This having been declared and having spoken he rushes headlong and wends his way towards a vacant and a free place and seat.

Two hours after and a-hundred-and-twenty minutes later, I meet him and see him again in the Cour de Rome and in front of the gare Saint-Lazare. He is with and in the company of a friend and pal who is advising and urging him to have a button and vegetable ivory disc added and sewn on to his overcoat and mantle.

itotes

Some of us were travelling together. A young man, who didn't look very intelligent, spoke to the man next to him for a few moments, then he went and sat down. Two hours later I met him again; he was with a friend and was talking about clothes.

etaphorically

In the centre of the day, tossed among the shoal of travelling sardines in a coleopter with a big white carapace, a chicken with a long, featherless neck suddenly harangued one, a peace-abiding one, of their number, and its parlance, moist with protest, was unfolded upon the airs. Then, attracted by a void, the fledgling precipitated itself thereunto.

In a bleak, urban desert, I saw it again that selfsame day, drinking the cup of humiliation offered by a lowly button.

Retrograde

You ought to put another button on your over-coat, his friend told him. I met him in the middle of the Cour de Rome, after having left him rushing avidly towards a seat. He had just protested against being pushed by another passenger who, he said, was jostling him every time anyone got off. This scraggy young man was the wearer of a ridiculous hat. This took place on the platform of an S bus which was full that particular midday.

urprises

How tightly packed in we were on that bus platform! And how stupid and ridiculous that young man looked! And what was he doing? Well, if he wasn't actually trying to pick a quarrel with a chap who—so he claimed! the young fop! kept on pushing him! And then he didn't find anything better to do than to rush off and grab a seat which had become free! Instead of leaving it for a lady!

Two hours after, guess whom I met in front of the gare Saint-Lazare! The same fancy-pants! Being given some sartorial advice! By a friend!

You'd never believe it!

26

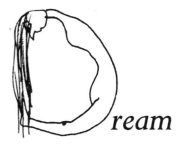ream

I had the impression that everything was misty and nacreous around me, with multifarious and indistinct apparitions, amongst whom however was one figure that stood out fairly clearly which was that of a young man whose too-long neck in itself seemed to proclaim the character at once cowardly and quarrelsome of the individual. The ribbon of his hat had been replaced by a piece of plaited string. Later he was having an argument with a person whom I couldn't see and then, as if suddenly afraid, he threw himself into the shadow of a corridor.

Another part of the dream showed him walking in bright sunshine in front of the gare Saint-Lazare. He was with a companion who was saying: "You ought to have another button put on your overcoat."

Whereupon I woke up.

rognostication

When midday strikes you will be on the rear platform of a bus which will be crammed full of passengers amongst whom you will notice a ridiculous juvenile; skeleton-like neck and no ribbon on his felt hat. He don't be feeling at his ease, poor little chap. He will think that a gentleman is pushing him on purpose every time that people getting on or off pass by. He will tell him so but the gentleman won't deign to answer. And the ridiculous juvenile will be panic-stricken and run away from him in the direction of a vacant seat.

You will see him a little later, in the Cour de

Rome in front of the gare Saint-Lazare. A friend will be with him and you will hear these words: "Your overcoat doesn't do up properly; you must have another button put on it."

ynchysis

Ridiculous young man, as I was on an S bus one day chock-full by traction perhaps whose neck was elongated, round his hat and who had a cord, I noticed a. Arrogant and snivelling in a tone, who happened to be next to him, with the man to remonstrate he started. Because that he pushed him he claimed, time every that got off anyone. Vacant he sat down and made a dash towards a seat, having said this. Rome (Cour de) in the I met him later two hours to his overcoat a button to add a friend was advising him.

The rainbow

One day I happened to be on the platform of a violet bus. There was a rather ridiculous young man on it—indigo neck, cord round his hat. All of a sudden he started to remonstrate with a blue man. He charged him in particular, in a green voice, with jostling him every time anybody got off. Having said this, he rushed headlong towards a yellow seat and sat down on it.

Two hours later I saw him in front of an orange-coloured station. He was with a friend who was advising him to have another button put on his red overcoat.

ord game

(Dowry, bayonet, enemy, chapel, atmosphere,
Bastille, correspondence)

One day I happened to be on the platform of
a bus which must no doubt have formed part
of the dowry of the daughter of a gentleman
called Monsieur Mariage who presided over
the destinies of the Paris Passenger Transport
Board. There was a young man on this bus
who was rather ridiculous, not because he
wasn't carrying a bayonet, but because he
looked as if he was carrying one when all the
time he wasn't carrying one. All of a sudden
this young man attacked his enemy—a man

standing behind him. He accused him in particular of not behaving as politely as one would in a chapel. Having thus strained the atmosphere, the little squirt went and sat down.

Two hours later I met him two or three kilometres from the Bastille with a friend who was advising him to have an extra button put on his overcoat, an opinion which he could very well have given him by correspondence.

Hesitation

I don't really know where it happened . . . in a church, a dustbin, a charnel-house? A bus, perhaps? There were . . . but what were there, though? Eggs, carpets, radishes? Skeletons? Yes, but with their flesh still round them, and alive. I think that's how it was. People in a bus. But one (or two?) of them was making himself conspicuous, I don't really know in what way. For his megalomania? For his adiposity? For his melancholy? Rather . . . more precisely . . . for his youth, which was embellished by a long . . . nose? chin? thumb? no: neck, and by a strange, strange, strange hat. He started to quarrel, yes, that's right.

35

with, no doubt, another passenger (man or woman? child or old age pensioner?) This ended, this finished by ending in a commonplace sort of way, probably by the flight of one of the two adversaries.

I rather think that it was the same character I met, but where? In front of a church? in front of a charnel-house? in front of a dustbin? With a friend who must have been talking to him about something, but about what? about what? about what?

Precision

In a bus of the S-line, 10 metres long, 3 wide, 6 high, at 3 km. 600 m. from its starting point, loaded with 48 people, at 12.17 p.m., a person of the masculine sex aged 27 years 3 months and 8 days, 1 m. 72 cm. tall and weighing 65 kg. and wearing a hat 35 cm. in height round the crown of which was a ribbon 60 cm. long, interpellated a man aged 48 years 4 months and 3 days, 1 m. 68 cm. tall and weighing 77 kg., by means of 14 words whose enunciation lasted 5 seconds and which alluded to some involuntary displacements of from 15 to 20 mm. Then he went and sat down about 1 m. 10 cm. away.

57 minutes later he was 10 metres away from the suburban entrance to the gare Saint-Lazare and was walking up and down over a distance of 30 m. with a friend aged 28, 1 m. 70 cm. tall and weighing 71 kg. who advised him in 15 words to move by 5 cm. in the direction of the zenith a button which was 3 cm. in diameter.

The subjective side

I was not displeased with my attire this day. I was inaugurating a new, rather sprightly hat, and an overcoat of which I thought most highly. Met X in front of the gare Saint-Lazare who tried to spoil my pleasure by trying to prove that this overcoat is cut too low at the lapels and that I ought to have an extra button on it. At least he didn't dare attack my head-gear.

A bit earlier I had roundly told off a vulgar type who was purposely ill-treating me every time anyone went by getting off or on. This happened in one of those unspeakably foul

omnibi which fill up with hoi polloi precisely
at those times when I have to consent to use
them.

nother subjectivity

Next to me on the bus platform today there was one of those half-baked young fellows, you don't find so many of them these days, thank God, otherwise I should end up by killing one. This particular one, a brat of something like 26 or 30, irritated me particularly not so much because of his great long featherless-turkey's neck as because of the nature of the ribbon round his hat, a ribbon which wasn't much more than a sort of marooncoloured string. Dirty beast! He absolutely disgusted me! As there were a lot of people in our bus at that hour I took advantage of all the pushing and shoving there is every time anyone gets on or off to dig him in the ribs with my elbow. In the end he took to his heels, the milksop, before I could make up my mind to tread on his dogs to teach him a lesson. I could also have told him, just to annoy him, that he needed another button on his overcoat which was cut too low at the lapels.

Narrative

One day at about midday in the Parc Monceau district, on the back platform of a more or less full S bus (now No. 84), I observed a person with a very long neck who was wearing a felt hat which had a plaited cord round it instead of a ribbon. This individual suddenly addressed the man standing next to him, accusing him of purposely treading on his toes every time any passengers got on or off. However he quickly abandoned the dispute and threw himself on to a seat which had become vacant.

Two hours later I saw him in front of the gare Saint-Lazare engaged in earnest conversation with a friend who was advising him to reduce the space between the lapels of his overcoat by getting a competent tailor to raise the top button.

W ord-composition

I was plat-bus-forming co-massitudinarily in a lutetio-meridional space-time and I was neighbouring a longisthmusical plaitroundthehatted greenhorn. Who said to a mediocranon: "You're jostleseeming me." Having ejaculated this he freeplaced himself voraciously. In a posterior spatio-temporality I saw him again; he was saint-lazaresquaring with an X who was saying: "You ought to buttonsupplement your overcoat." And he whyexplained him.

Negativities

It was neither a boat, nor an aeroplane, but a terrestrial means of transport. It was neither the morning, nor the evening, but midday. It was neither a baby, nor an old man, but a young man. It was neither a ribbon, nor a string, but a plaited cord. It was neither a procession, nor a brawl, but a scuffle. It was neither a pleasant person, nor an evil person, but a bad-tempered person. It was neither a truth, nor a lie, but a pretext. It was neither a standing person, nor a recumbent person, but a would-be-seated person.

It was neither the day before, nor the day after,

but the same day. It was neither the gare du Nord, nor the gare du P.-L.-M. but the gare Saint-Lazare. It was neither a relation, nor a stranger, but a friend. It was neither insult, nor ridicule, but sartorial advice.

nimism

A soft, brown hat with a dent in his middle, his brim turned down, a plaited cord round his crown, one hat among many others, jumping only when the bumps in the road were transmitted to him by the wheels of the automobile vehicle which was transporting him (the hat). At each stop the comings and goings of the passengers caused him to make certain lateral movements which at times were fairly pronounced, and this ended by angering him (the hat). He expressed his ire by the intermediary of a human voice which was attached to him by a mass of flesh structurally disposed round a sort of bony sphere perforated by a

48

few holes, which was situated below him (the hat). Then he (the hat) suddenly went and sat down.

One or two hours later I saw him (the hat) again, moving about at roughly 1m. 66cm. above the ground and up and down in front of the gare Saint-Lazare. A friend was advising him to an extra button put on his overcoat . . . an extra button . . . on his overcoat . . . to tell him that . . . him . . . (the hat).

nagrams

In het S sub in het hurs hour a pach of tabou swinettyx, who had a glon, hint cken and a tah mmitred with a droc instead of a borbin, had an urmagent with athrone gaspenser whom he uccased of stoljing him on sporeup. Having had a good oman he dame a shad orf a feer teas.

An hour trale I emt him in het Cuor ed More, in norft of het rage Tsian-Zalare. He saw with a refind who was yasing to him: "You tough to heav an artex tutnob upt on your oectrova." He woshed him hewer (at het peninog.)

50

Distinguo

In an S bus (which is not to be confused with a trespass), I saw (not an eyesore) a chap (not a Bath one) wearing a dark soft hat (and not a hot daft sack), which hat was encircled by a plaited cord (and not by an applauded cat). One of his characteristics (and not his character's instincts) was a prim neck (and not a numb prick). As the people were pushing and shoving (and not the sheep were shooshing and pupping), a newcomer (not a cute number) displaced the latter (not lacerated the display). The chap complained (not the chaplain comped), but seeing a free place (not placing a free See) made a bee-line for it (not bade me lie in for it).

Later I perceived him (not high Erse peeved
'im) in front of the gare Saint-Lazare (and not
the lass in Gaza). He was talking to a friend
(and not trending to a fork) about a button on
his coat (which is not to be confused with a
cut on—?—on his boat.)

Homeoptotes

On a certain date, a corporate crate on which the electorate congregate when they migrate at a great rate, late, had to accommodate an ornate, tracheate celibate, who started to altercate with a proximate inmate, and ejaculate: "Mate, why do you lacerate, obliterate and excoriate my plates?" But to anticipate Billingsgate debate, he hastened to abdicate, and sate.

An houate aftrate, in front of the Saint-Lazate gate, I notate him agate, talkate about a buttate, a buttate on his overcate.

Official letter

I beg to advise you of the following facts
of which I happened to be the equally
impartial and horrified witness.

Today, at roughly twelve noon, I was present
on the platform of a bus which was proceeding up the rue de Courcelles in the direction
of the Place Champerret. The aforementioned
bus was fully laden - more than fully
laden, I might even ventureto say, since
the conductor had accepted an overload of
several candidates, without valid reason
and actuated by an exaggerated kindness of
heart which caused him to exceed the regu-
lations and which, consequently, bordered
on indulgence. At each stopping place the

perambulations of the outgoing and
incoming passengers did not fail to provoke
a certain disturbance which incited one
of these passengers to protest, though not
without timidity. I should mention that
he went and sat down as and when this
eventuality became possible.

I will append to this short account this
addendum: I had occasion to observe this
passenger some time subsequently in the
company of an individual whom I was unable
to identify. The conversation which they
were exchanging with some animation seemed
to have a bearing on questions of an aesthetic
nature.

In view of these circumstances, I would
request you to be so kind, Sir, as to intimate
to me the inference which I should draw
from these facts and the attitude which you
would then deem appropriate that I adopt
in re the conduct of my subsequent mode of
life.

Anticipating the favour of your reply,
believe me to be, Sir, your very obedient
servant at least.

lurb

In this new novel, executed with his accustomed *brio*, the famous novelist X, to whom we are already indebted for so many masterpieces, has decided to confine himself to very clear-cut characters who act in an atmosphere which everybody, both adults and children, can understand. The plot revolves, then, round the meeting in a bus of the hero of this story and of a rather enigmatic character who picks a quarrel with the first person he meets. In the final episode we see this mysterious individual listening with the greatest attention to the advice of a friend, a past master of Sartorial Art. The whole makes a charming impression which the novelist X has etched with rare felicity.

nomatopoeia

On the platform, pla pla pla, of a bus, chuff chuff chuff, which was an S (and singing still dost soar, and soaring ever singest), it was about noon, ding dang dong, ding dang dong, a ridiculous ephebus, poof poof, who had one of those hats, pooh, suddenly turned (twirl twirl) on his neighbour angrily, grrh grrh, and said, hm hm : "You are purposely jostling me, Sir," Ha ha. Whereupon, phfftt, he threw himself on to a free seat and sat down, plonk.

The same day, a bit later, ding dang dong, ding dang dong, I saw him again in the company of another ephebus, poof poof, who was talking

58

overcoat buttons, (boorra boorra, it wasn't as
warm as all that . . .)

Ha ha.

logical analysis

Bus.
Platform.
Bus platform. That's the place.
Midday.
About.
About midday. That's the time.
Passengers.
Quarrel.
A passengers' quarrel. That's the action.
Young man.
Hat. Long thin neck.
A young man with a hat and a plaited cord
   round it. That's the chief character.
Person.

A person.
A person. That's the second character.
Me.
Me.
Me. That's the third character, narrator.
Words.
Words.
Words. That's what was said.
Seat vacant.
Seat taken.
A seat that was vacant and then taken. That's the result.
The gare Saint-Lazare.
An hour later.
A friend.
A button.
Another phrase heard. That's the conclusion.
Logical conclusion.

Insistence

One day, at about midday, I got into an S bus which was nearly full. In an S bus which was nearly full there was a rather ridiculous young man. I got into the same bus as he, and this young man, having got into this same nearly full S bus before me, at about 12 noon, was wearing on his head a hat which I found highly ridiculous, I, the person who happened to be in the same bus as he, on the S line, one day, at about 12 noon.

This hat was encircled by a sort of lanyard-like plaited cord, and the young man who was wearing the hat—and the cord—happened to be in the same bus as I, a bus which was nearly full because it was 12 noon; and underneath the hat, whose cord was an imitation of a lanyard, was a face succeeded by a long neck, by a long, long neck. Ah, how long it was, the neck of the young man who was wearing a hat encircled by a lanyard on an S bus, one day at about 12 noon.

There was a lot of pushing and shoving in the bus which was conveying us towards the terminus of the S line, one day at about 12 noon, me and the young man who had put a long neck under a ridiculous hat. The jolts which occurred resulted in a protest, which protest emanated from the young man who had such a long neck on the platform of an S bus, one day at about 12 noon.

There was an accusation formulated in a voice damp with wounded dignity, because on the platform of an S bus, a young man had a hat which was equipped with a lanyard all the way round it, and a long neck; there was also a vacant seat suddenly in this S bus which was nearly full because it was 12 noon, a seat which was soon occupied by the young man with the long neck and the ridiculous hat, a seat which he coveted because he didn't wish to get pushed around any more on that bus platform, one day at about 12 noon.

Two hours later I saw him again in front of the gare Saint-Lazare, the young man whom I had noticed on the platform of an S bus, the same day, at about 12 noon. He was with a companion of the same species as himself who was giving him some advice relative to a certain button on his overcoat. The other was listening attentively. The other—that's the young man who had a lanyard round his hat, and whom I saw on the platform of a nearly full S bus, one day, at about 12 noon.

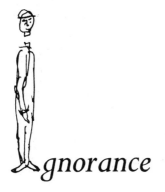

gnorance

Personally I don't know what they want of me. Yes, I got on an S bus about midday. Were there a lot of people? Of course there were, at that hour. A young man with a felt hat? It's quite possible. Personally I don't examine people under a microscope. I don't give a damn. A kind of plaited cord? Round his hat? I'll agree that's a bit peculiar, but it doesn't strike me personally as anything else. A plaited cord . . . He had words with another man? There's nothing unusual about that.

And then I saw him again an hour or two later? Why not? There are a lot of things

in life that are more peculiar than that. For
instance, I remember my father was always
telling me about . . .

ast

I got into the Porte Champerret bus. There were a lot of people in it, young, old, women, soldiers. I paid for my ticket and then looked around me. It wasn't very interesting. But finally I noticed a young man whose neck I thought was too long. I examined his hat and I observed that instead of a ribbon it had a plaited cord. Every time another passenger got on there was a lot of pushing and shoving. I didn't say anything, but all the same the young man with the long neck started to quarrel with his neighbour. I didn't hear what he said, but they gave each other some dirty looks. Then the young man with the long neck went and sat down in a hurry.

Coming back from the Porte Champerret I passed in front of the gare Saint-Lazare. I saw my young man having a discussion with a pal. the pal indicated a button just above the lapels of the young man's overcoat. Then the bus took me off and I didnt see them any more. I had a seat and I wasn't thinking about anything.

_P_resent

At midday the heat coils round the feet of bus passengers. If, placed on a long neck, a stupid head adorned with a grotesque hat should chance to become inflamed, then a quarrel immediately breaks out. Very soon to become dissipated, however, in an atmosphere too heavy to carry ultimate insults very vividly from mouth to ear.

Thus one goes and sits down inside, where it's cool.

Later can be posed, in front of stations with double courtyards, sartorial questions about some button or other which fingers slimy with sweat self-confidently fiddle with.

Reported speech

Dr. Queneau said that it had happened at mid-day. Some passengers had got into the bus. They had been squashed tightly together. On his head a young man had been wearing a hat which had been encircled by a plait and not by a ribbon. He had had a long neck. He had complained to the man standing next to him about the continual jostling which the latter had been inflicting on him. As soon as he had noticed a vacant seat, said Dr. Queneau, the young man had rushed off towards it and sat down upon it.

He had seen him later, Dr. Queneau continued,

in front of the gare Saint-Lazare. He had been wearing an overcoat, and a friend who had happened to be present had made a remark to him to the effect that he ought to put an extra button on the said overcoat.

assive

It was midday. The bus was being got into by passengers. They were being squashed together. A hat was being worn on the head of a young gentleman, which hat was encircled by a plait and not by a ribbon. A long neck was one of the characteristics of the young gentleman. The man standing next to him was being grumbled at by the latter because of the jostling which was being inflicted on him by him. As soon as a vacant seat was espied by the young gentleman it was made the object of his precipitate movements and it became sat down upon.

The young gentleman was later seen by me in front of the gare Saint-Lazare. He was clothed in an overcoat and was having a remark made to him by a friend who happened to be there to the effect that it was necessary to have an extra button put on it.

lexandrines

One midday in the bus—the S-line was its ilk—
I saw a little runt, a miserable milk—
Sop, voicing discontent, although around his
    turban
He had a plaited cord, this fancy-pants subur-
    ban.
Now hear what he complained of, this worm-
    metamorphosis
With disproportionate neck, suffering from
    halitosis:
—A citizen standing near him who'd come to
    man's estate
Was constantly refusing to circumnavigate
His toes, each time a chap got in the bus and
    rode,

74

Panting, and late for lunch, towards his chaste
   abode.
But scandal was there none; this sorry personage
Espied a vacant seat—made thither quick
   pilgrimage.
As I was going back towards the Latin Quarter
I saw him once again, this youth of milk-and-
   water.
And heard his foppish friend telling him with
   dispassion :
"The opening of your coat is not the latest
   fashion."

olyptotes

I got into a bus full of taxpayers who were giving some money to a taxpayer who had on his taxpayer's stomach a little box which allowed the other taxpayers to continue their taxpayers' journeys. I noticed in this bus a taxpayer with a long taxpayer's neck and whose taxpayer's head bore a taxpayer's felt hat encircled by a plait the like of which no taxpayer ever wore before. Suddenly the said taxpayer peremptorily addressed a nearby taxpayer, complaining bitterly that he was purposely treading on his taxpayer's toes every time other taxpayers got on or off the taxpayers' bus. Then the angry taxpayer went

76

and sat down in a seat for taxpayers which another taxpayer had just vacated. Some taxpayer's hours later I caught sight of him in the Cour for the taxpayers de Rome, in the company of a taxpayer who was giving him some advice on the elegance of the taxpayer.

pheresis

Ot us sengers. Ticed ung an eck embled at affe
ring at ith ted ord. Ot gry nother senger plain-
ing rod oes very one n ut. Ent at own here as
ree eat.

Ing ack eft ank ticed king own ith riend ving
vice ow egant wing irst ton oat.

pocope

I g into a bu full of passen. I no a yo ma whose n resem th of a gir and who was wea a h w a plai cor. He g an with a passen, complai that he tr on his t e time any got i or o. Then he w and s d because th w a f s.

Go b l b, I no him wal up and d w a f who was gi him ad on h to be ele, sho him the f but of his c.

yncope

I gt io bs full opssgers. I niced a youngn with a nesemataraffe and with a hathaplord. He got angwer pssger because he comined that he troes. Then he occed a vnt st.

When I was ging along the sroute in the oppection, I niced him in Courome. He was beven a lon in egance weference ta bun.

Speaking personally

That's something I do understand; a chap who goes out of his way to tread on your dogs, it makes you bloody wild. But after you've made a fuss about it to go and sit down like a bloody coward, that personally I don't understand. I saw it with my own eyes the other day on the back platform of an S bus. Personally I thought the young man's neck was somewhat long and I also thought that kind of plait thing round his hat was bloody silly. Personally I would never dare to show myself in such a get-up. But anyway, like I said, when he'd moaned at another passenger who was treading on his toes, this chap went and sat down and that was that. Personally I would have clipped him one, any bastard that trod on my toes.

I tell you, personally I think there are some odd things in this life, it's only mountains that never meet. A couple of hours later I met that young chap again. I saw him with my own eyes in front of the gare Saint-Lazare. Yes, I saw him myself with a friend of his own kidney who was saying—I heard him with my own ears: "You ought to raise that button." I personally saw him with my own eyes, he was pointing to the top button.

Exclamations

Goodness! Twelve o'clock! time for the bus!
what a lot of people! what a lot of people!
aren't we squashed! bloody funny! that chap!
what a face! and what a neck! two-foot long!
at least! and the cord! the cord! I hadn't
seen it! the cord! that's the bloody funniest!
oh! the cord! round his hat! A cord! bloody
funny! too bloody funny! here we go, now
he's yammering! the chap with the cord! at
the chap next to him! what's he saying! The
other chap! claims he trod on his toes!
They're going to come to blows! definitely!
no, though! yes they are, though! go wonn!
go wonn! bite him in the eye! charge! hit

'im! well I never! no, though! he's climbing down! the chap! with the long neck! with the cord! it's a vacant seat he's charging! yes! the chap!

Well! 't's true! no! I'm right! it's really him! over there! in the Cour de Rome! in front of the gare Saint-Lazare! mooching up and down! with another chap! and what's the other chap telling him! that he ought to get an extra button! yes! a button on his coat! On his coat!

ou know

Well, *you* know, the bus arrived, so, *you* know,
I got on. Then I saw, *you* know, a citizen
who, *you know*, caught my eye, sort of. I
mean, *you* know, I saw his long neck and I
saw the plait round his hat. Then he started to,
you know, rave, at the chap next to him. He
was, *you* know, treading on his toes. Then he
went and, *you* know, sat down.

Well, *you* know, later on, I saw him in the
Cour de Rome. He was with a, *you* know,
pal, and he was telling him, *you* know, the pal
was: "You ought to get another button put on
your coat." *You* know.

oble

At the hour when the rosy fingers of the dawn start to crack I climbed, rapid as a tongue of flame, into a bus, mighty of stature and with cow-like eyes, of the S-line of sinuous course. I noticed, with the precision and acuity of a Red Indian on the warpath, the presence of a young man whose neck was longer than that of the swift-footed giraffe, and whose felt hat was adorned with a plait like the hero of an exercise in style. Baleful Discord with breasts of soot came with her mouth reeking of a nothingness of toothpaste, Discord, I say, came to breathe her malignant virus between this young man with the giraffe neck and the plait

86

round his hat, and a passenger of irresolute and farinaceous mien. The former addressed himself to the latter in these terms: "I say, you, anyone might think you were treading on my toes on purpose!" Having said these words, the young man with the giraffe neck and the plait round his hat quickly went and sat down.

Later, in the Cour de Rome of majestic proportions, I again caught sight of the young man with the giraffe neck and the plait round his hat, accompanied by a friend, an arbiter elegantiarum, who was uttering these words of censure which I could hear with my agile ear, censure which was directed to the most exterior garment of the young man with the giraffe neck and the plait round his hat: "You ought to diminish its opening by the addition or elevation of a button to or on its circular periphery."

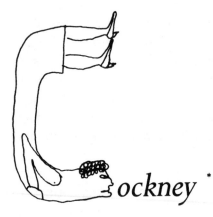

ockney *

So A'm stand'n' n' ahtsoider vis frog bus when A sees vis young Froggy bloke, caw bloimey, A finks, 'f'at ain't ve most funniest look'n' geezer wot ever A claps eyes on. Bleed'n' great neck, jus' loike a tellyscope, strai' up i' was, an' ve titfer 'e go' on 'is bonce, caw, A fought A'd 'a died. Six foot o' skin an' grief, A ses to meself, when awlver sud'n 'e starts to come ve ol' acid, an': "Gaw bloimey," 'e ses, "wot ver ber-lee-din' ow yeh fink yeh adeouin' of?" 'E's tawkin' to annuver bleed'n' fawrner vere on ve bus pla'form; ses 'e keeps a-treadin' on 'is plites awler toime, real narky 'e gets, till vis uvver Frog bloke turns roun' an'

88

ses : " 'Ere," 'e ses, "oo yeh fink yeh git'n' a'?
Garn," 'e ses, "A'll give yeh a pro'r mahrfful
na minute," 'e ses, "gi' ah a vit." So 'e does,
pore bastard, 'e does a bunk real quick deahn
ve bus wivaht anuvver word.

Cup lowers la'r, guess wo'? A sees ve fust
young bleeder agin walkin' up'n deahn ahtsoider ve Garsn Lazzer, arkin' to anuvver
young Froggy a-jorein' 'im abeaht a bleedin'
bu'en.

---

ross-examination

—At what time did the 12.23 p.m. S-line bus proceeding in the direction of the Porte de Champerret arrive on that day?
—At 12.38 p.m.
—Were there many people on the aforesaid S bus?
—Bags of 'em.
—Did you particularly notice any of them?
—An individual who had a very long neck and a plait round his hat.
—Was his demeanour as singular as his attire and his anatomy?
—At the very beginning, no; it was normal, but in the end it proved to be that of a slightly

90

hypotonic paranoiac cyclothymic in a state of hypergastric irritability.

—How did that become apparent?

—The individual in question interpellated the man next to him and asked him in a whining tone if he was not making a point of treading on his toes every time any passengers got on or off.

—Had this reproach any foundation?

—I've no idea.

—How did the incident terminate?

—By the precipitate flight of the young man who went to occupy a vacant seat.

—Was there any sequel to this incident?

—Less than two hours later.

—In what did this sequel consist?

—In the reappearance of this person across my path.

—Where and how did you see him again?

—When I was passing the Cour de Rome in a bus.

—What was he doing there?

—He was being given some sartorial advice.

omedy

ACT ONE
SCENE 1
On the back platform of an S bus, one day,
round about 12 noon.

THE CONDUCTOR : Fez pliz. (*Some passengers*
hand him their fares.)

SCENE 2
(*The bus stops*)

THE CONDUCTOR : Let 'em off first. Any priori-
ties? One priority! Full up. Dring dring
dring.

92

ACT TWO
SCENE 1

(*Same set.*)

FIRST PASSENGER : (*young, long neck, a plait round his hat*) It seems, Sir, that you make a point of treading on my toes every time anyone goes by.

SECOND PASSENGER : (*shrugs his shoulders*)

SCENE 2

(*A third passenger gets off*)

FIRST PASSENGER: (*to the audience*) Whacko! a free seat! I'll get it before anyone else does. (*He precipitates himself on to it and occupies if*)

ACT THREE
SCENE 1

(*The Cour de Rome*)

A YOUNG DANDY : (*to the first passenger, now a pedestrian*) The opening of your overcoat is too wide. You ought to make it a bit narrower by having the top button raised.

SCENE 2

On the S bus, passing the Cour de Rome.

FOURTH PASSENGER : Huh, the chap who was in the bus with me earlier on and who was

93

having a row with another chap.   Odd
encounter.   I'll make it into a comedy in
three acts and in prose.

sides

The bus arrived bulging with passengers. *Only hope I don't miss it, oh good, there's still just room for me.* One of them *queer sort of mug he's got with that enormous neck* was wearing a soft felt hat with a sort of little plait round it instead of a ribbon *just showing off that is* and suddenly started *hey what's got into him* to vituperate his neighbour *the other chap isn't taking any notice of him* reproaching him for deliberately treading *seems as if he's looking for trouble but he'll climb down* on his toes. But as there was a free seat inside *didn't I say so* he turned his back and made haste to occupy it.

About two hours later *coincidences are peculiar* he was in the Cour de Rome with a friend *a fancy-pants of his own sort* who was pointing with his index finger to a button on his overcoat *what on earth can he be telling him?*

arechesis

On the butt-end of a bulging bus which was transbustling an abundance of incubuses and Buchmanites from bumbledom towards their bungalows, a bumptious buckeen whose buttocks were remote from his bust and who was buttired in a boody ridiculous busby, buddenly had a bust-up with a robust buckra who was bumping into him: "Buccaneer, buzz off, you're butting my bunions!" Rebuffed, he did a bunk.

But bussequently I buheld him with a buckish buddy who was busuading him to budge a button on his bum-freezer.

Spectral

We, gamekeeper of the Monceau Plain, have
the honour to report the inexplicable and
malignant presence in the neighbourhood of
the oriental gate of the Park, property of his
Royal Highness Monsieur Philippe, the in-
vested Duke of Orleans, this sixteenth day of
May one thousand seven hundred and eighty
three, of a felt hat of an unwonted shape and
encircled by a sort of plaited cord. We subsequently observed the sudden apparition
under the said hat of a man who was young,
endowed with a neck of an extraordinary
length, and dressed how they dress, doubtless,
in China. The appalling aspect of this indivi-

dual froze our blood and prevented our flight. This individual remained immobile for several instants, and then began to make agitated movements, muttering the while, as if pushing aside other individuals in his vicinity who were invisible but perceptible to him. Suddenly he transferred his attention to his cloak and we heard him murmuring as follows: "A button is missing, a button is missing." Then he started to move and took the direction of the Nursery Garden. Attracted in spite of ourself by the strangeness of this phenomenon, we followed him out of the confines attributed to our jurisdiction and we all three, we, the individual and the hat, reached a deserted little garden, which was planted with cabbages. A blue sign of unknown but certainly diabolical origin bore the inscription "Cour de Rome". The individual continued to move about for some moments, murmuring: "He tried to tread on my toes." Then he disappeared, first himself, and, some time after, his hat. Having drawn up a report of this liquidation, I went to have a drink at the Little Poland.

$\mathcal{P}$hilosophic

Great cities alone can provide phenomenological spirituality with the essentialities of temporal and improbabilistic coincidences. The philosopher who occasionally ascends into the futile and utilitarian inexistentiality of an S bus can perceive therein with the lucidity of his pineal eye the transitory and faded appearance of a profane consciousness afflicted by the long neck of vanity and the hatly plait of ignorance. This matter, void of true entelechy, occasionally plunges into the categorical imperative of its recriminatory life force against the neo-Berkleyan unreality of a corporeal mechanism unburdened by conscience. This moral attitude then carries the more unconscious of the two towards a void spatiality where it disintegrates into its primary and crooked elements.

Philosophical research is then pursued normally by the fortuitous but anagogic encounter of the same being accompanied by its inessential and sartorial replica, which is noumenally advising it to transpose on the level of the understanding the concept of overcoat button situated sociologically too low.

Apostrophe

O platinum-nibbed stylograph, let thy smooth and rapid course trace on this single-side calendered paper those alphabetic glyphs which shall transmit to men of sparkling spectacles the narcissistic tale of a double encounter of omnibusilistic cause. Proud courser of my dreams, faithful camel of my literary exploits, lissome fountain of words counted, weighed and chosen, describe thou those lexicographic and syntactic curves which shall graphically create the futile and ridiculous narration of the life and opinions of that young man who one day took the S bus without suspecting that he would become the immortal hero of the present writer's laborious toil. O coxcomb with thy plait-girdled hat projecting over thy long neck, O cross-grained, choleric and pusillanimous cur who, fleeing the skirmish, wentest to place thy behind, harvester of kicks on the arse, on a bench of hardened wood, didst thou suspect this thy rhetorical destiny whilst, before the gare Saint-Lazare, thou wast listening with exalted ear to the tailoring counsel of a personage inspired by the uppermost button of thine overcoat?

Awkward

I'm not used to writing. I dunno. I'd quite like to write a tragedy or a sonnet or an ode, but there's the rules. They put me off. They weren't made for amateurs. All this is already pretty badly written. Oh well. At any rate, I saw something today which I'd like to set down in writing. Set down in writing doesn't seem all that marvellous to me. It's probably one of those ready-made expressions which are objected to by the readers who read for the publishers who are looking for the originality which they seem to think is necessary in the manuscripts which the publishers publish when they've been read by the readers who object to ready-made expressions like "to set down in writing" which all the same is what I should like to do about something I saw today even though I'm only an amateur who is put off by the rules of the tragedy the sonnet or the ode because I'm not used to writing. Hell, I don't know how I did it but here I am right back at the beginning again. I'll never get to the end. So what. Let's take the bull by the horns. Another platitude. And anyway there was nothing of the bull about that chap. Huh, that's not bad. If I were to write: let's take the fancy-pants by the plait of his felt hat which hat is conjugated with a long neck, that might well be original. That might well get me in with the gentlemen of the French Academy, the Café Flore and the Librairie Gallimard. Why shouldn't I make some progress, after all. It's by writing that you become a writesmith. That's a good one. Have to keep a sense of proportion, though. The chap on the bus platform had lost his when he started to swear at the man next to him claiming that the latter trod on his toes every time he squeezed himself up to let passengers get on or off. All the more so as after he'd protested in this fashion he went off quickly enough to sit down as soon as he'd spotted a free seat inside as if he was afraid of getting hit. Hm, I've got through half my story already. Wonder how I did it. Writing's really quite pleasant. But there's still the most difficult part left. The part where you need the most know-how. The transition. All the more so as there isn't any transition. I'd rather stop here.

asual

I

I get on the bus.
"Is this right for the Porte Champerret?"
"Cantcher read?"
"Pardon."
He grinds my tickets on his stomach.
"Ee yar."
"Thanks."
I look around me.
"I say, you."
He has a sort of cord round his hat.
"Can't you look what you're doing?"
He has a very long neck.
"Oh look here, I say."

Now he's rushing to get a free seat.
"Well well."
I say that to myself.

II

I get in the bus.
"Is this right for the Place de la Contrescarpe?"
"Cantcher read?"
"Pardon."
His barrel organ functions and gives me back
my tickets with a little tune on them.
"Ee yar.'
"Thanks."
We pass the gare Saint-Lazare.
"Hm, there's the chap I saw before."
I incline an ear.
"You ought to get another button put on your
overcoat."
He shows him where.
"Your overcoat is cut too low."
That's true enough.
"Well well."
I say that to myself.

iased

After an inordinate delay the bus at last turned
the corner and pulled up alongside the pavement. A few people got off, a few others got
on. I was among the latter. I got shoved on
to the platform, the conductor vehemently
pulled a noise-plug and the vehicle started off
again. While I was engaged in tearing out of
a little book the number of tickets that the
man with the little box was about to obliterate
on his stomach, I started to inspect my neigh-
bours. Nothing but males around me. No
women. A disinterested look, then. I soon
discovered the cream of this surrounding mud:
a boy of about twenty who wore a little head

on a long neck and a large hat on his little head and a pretty little plait round his large hat.

What a ghastly type, I said to myself.

He wasn't only a ghastly type, he was a quarrelsome one as well. He worked himself up into a state of indignation and accused a perfectly ordinary citizen of laminating his feet every time a passenger went by getting on or off. The other fellow looked at him severely, trying to find an aggressive retort in the ready-made repertory that he no doubt lugged around with him through the varying circumstances of Life, but he was somewhat out of his depth that day. As for the young man, he was afraid he was going to get his face slapped, so he took advantage of the sudden liberation of a seat by precipitating himself upon it and sitting on it.

I got off before he did and couldn't continue to observe his behaviour. I was deciding to condemn him to oblivion when, two hours later, me in the bus, him on the pavement, I saw him in the Cour de Rome, looking just as deplorable.

He was walking up and down in the company of a friend who must have been his arbiter of elegance and who was advising him, with dandyesque pedantry, to reduce the space between the lapels of his overcoat by having a supplementary button united to it.

What a ghastly type, I said to myself.

Then the two of us, my bus and I, continued on our way.

Sonnet

Glabrous was his dial and plaited was his
 bonnet,
And he, a puny colt—(how sad the neck he
 bore,
And long)—was now intent on his quotidian
 chore—
The bus arriving full, of somehow getting on
 it.

One came, a number ten—or else perhaps an S,
Its platform, small adjunct of this plebeian
 carriage,
Was crammed with such a mob as to preclude
 free passage;
Rich bastards lit cigars upon it, to impress.

The young giraffe described so well in my first
    strophe,
Having got on the bus, started at once to curse
    an
Innocent citizen—(he wanted an easy trophy

But got the worst of it.)   Then, spying a vacant
    place,
Escaped thereto.   Time passed.   On the way
    back, a person
Was telling him that a button was just too
    low in space.

lfactory

In that meridian S, apart from the habitual smell, there was a smell of a beastly seedy ego, of effrontery, of jeering, of H-bombs, of a high jakes, of cakes and ale, of emanations, of opium, of curious ardent esquimos, of tumescent venal double-usurers, of extraordinary white zoosperms, there was a certain scent of long juvenile neck, a certain perspiration of plaited cord, a certain pungency of anger, a certain loose and constipated stench, which were so unmistakeable that when I passed the gare Saint-Lazare two hours later I recognised them and identified them in the cosmetic, modish and tailoresque perfume which emanated from a badly placed button.

114

ustatory

This particular bus had a certain taste. Curious, but undeniable. All buses don't have the same taste. That's often said, but it's true. Just try the experiment. This one—an S, not to make too great a mystery of it—had the suspicion of a flavour of grilled peanuts, not to go into too great detail. The platform had its own special bouquet, peanuts not just grilled but trodden as well. One metre 60 above the trampolin, a gourmand, only there wasn't one there, would have been able to taste something rather sourish which was the neck of a man of about thirty. And twenty centimetres higher still, the refined palate was offered the rare opportunity of sampling a plaited cord just slightly tinged with the flavour of cocoa. Next we sampled the chewing gum of dispute, the chestnuts of irritation, the grapes of wrath and a bunch of bitterness.

Two hours later we were entitled to the dessert : an overcoat button . . . a real delicacy.

actile

Buses are soft to the touch especially if you take them between the thighs and caress them with both hands, from the head towards the tail, from the engine towards the platform. But when you find yourself on this platform, then you perceive something rougher and harsher which is the bar or hand-rail, and sometimes something rounder and more elastic which is a buttock. Sometimes there are two of these and then you put the sentence into the plural. You can also take hold of a tubular, palpitating object that disgurgitates idiotic sounds, or even a utensil with plaited spirals that are softer than a rosary, silkier than barbed wire, more

117

velvety than rope, and slenderer than a cable. Or your finger can even touch human clottishness, slightly viscous and gummy on account of the heat.

Then if you are patient for an hour or two, in front of a bumpy station you can dip your tepid hand into the exquisite freshness of a vegetable ivory button which is not in its right place.

*V*isual

The general effect is green with a white top, oblong, with windows. 'Tisn't as easy as all that to do windows. The platform isn't any colour, it's half grey half brown if it must be something. The most important thing is it's full of curves, lots of esses as you might say. But the way it is at midday, rush hour, it's an extraordinary mess. To get somewhere near it you'd have to extract from the magma a light ochre rectangle, put a light ochre oval on top, and then on top of that again, stick a darkish ochre hat which you'd encircle with a plait of burnt Siena, all mixed-up, at that. Then you'd shove in a patch the colour of

119

duck's muck to represent fury, a red triangle to express anger, and just a pissworth of green to portray suppressed bile and squittery funk.

After that you'd draw one of those sweet darling little navy blue overcoats and, near the top of it, just below the opening, you'd put a darling little button drawn with great precision and loving care.

uditory

Quacking and letting off, the S came rasping to a halt alongside the silent pavement. The sun's trombone flattened the midday note. The pedestrians, bawling bagpipes, shouted out their numbers. Some went up a semitone, which sufficed to carry them off towards the Porte Champerret with its chanting arcades. Among the panting élite was a clarinet tube to whom the untowardness of the times had given human form, and the perversity of a hatmaker had given to wear on the coconut an instrument which resembled a guitar that might perhaps have plaited its strings together to make a girdle. Suddenly in the middle of

121

some minor arrangements between enterprising passengers and consenting passengeresses and of bleating tremolos from the covetous conductor, a ludicrous cacophony broke out in which the fury of the double bass was blended with the irritation of the trumpet and the jitters of the bassoon.

Then, after sigh, silence, pause and double pause, there rang forth the triumphant melody of a button in the process of going up an octave.

elegraphic

BUS CROWDED STOP YNGMAN LONGNECK
PLAITENCIRCLED HAT APOSTROPHISES
UNKNOWN PASSENGER UNAPPARENT
REASON STOP QUERY FINGERS FEET HURT
CONTACT HEEL ALLEGED PURPOSELY STOP
YNGMAN ABANDONS DISCUSSION PRO-
VACANT SEAT STOP 1400 HOURS PLACE
ROME YNGMAN LISTENS SARTORIAL
ADVICE FRIEND STOP MOVE BUTTON STOP
SIGNED ARCTURUS

de

O in the bus
O in the bin
th'yomnibus S
th'yomnibussin
which with percuss
and hellish din
goes on its way
with us within
nearth' Parc Monceau
nearth' Parc Monsin
in the sun's glow
in the sun's glin
Monsieur André
whose neck's too thin

125

wears a hatuss
wears a hatin
in th'yomnibus
in th'yomnibin

And this hatuss
and this hatin
is ribbonless
is ribbonlin
in th'yomnibus
in th'yomnibin
and what is muss
and what is min
there's an excess
of bods therein
and this André
whose neck's too thin
starts to inveigh
starts to invin
against a cuss
against a kin
in th'yomnibus
in th'yomnibin
but this same cuss
but this same kin
za bit too tuss
za bit too tin
and says his say

126

and says his sin
on th'yomnibus
on th'yomnibin

and our André
whose neck's too thin
goes by express
goes by exprin
in the bus S
in the bussin
a seat to let
his arse sink in

A seat I'd let
my arse sink in
I the poet
gay Harlequin
and two hours a-
fter I saw him
at Saint-Lazare
at Saint-Lazin
the station? yeah
so spick and spin
him, that's André
whose neck's too thin
I heard him say
"O pardon min
my dear old pay

my dear old pin
for my buttuss
for my buttin"
quite near the bus
quite near the bin

Now if by cha-
ncetmy tale you grin
since happiness
was born a twin
then take no res-
tand take no rin
until from far
until from finn
from the bus S
from the bussin
you too your eyes
should chance to spin
on that André
whose neck's too thin
& his hatuss
& his hatin
& his buttuss
& his buttin
in th'yomnibus
in th'yomnibin
th'yomnibus S
th'yomnibussin.

128

Permutations by groups of 2, 3, 4 and 5 letters

Ed on to ay rd wa id sm yo da he nt ar re at
pl rm fo an of us sb aw is ou ay ma ng ho nw
ne se wa ck oo st ng lo dw an wa ho ea sw ng
ri at ah th wi la ap ro it dt un sa he me.

Den sud est lyh edt art ran oha his gue ghb
nei cla our ngt imi hew hat urp asp lyt ose din
rea his gon sev toe tim ery yon ean tin ego
ut oro.

Verh howe idly erap done aban disc dthe onan
ussi eada dmad rava shfo seat cant.

Oursl afewh sawhi ateri ninfr magai thega

ontof ntlaz resai gross areen conve edina onwit
rsati endwh hafri ellin owast ogett ghimt butto
hetop sover nofhi aised coatr.

Permutations by groups of 5, 6, 7 and 8 letters

Ytowa oneda ddayo rdsmi earpl nther mofan atfor saway sbusi anwho oungm kwast senec gandw oolon weari howas twith ngaha tedco aplai ndit rdrou. Lyhest sudden oharan artedt neighb guehis imingt ourcla urpose hathep onhist lytrod rytime oeseve gotino anyone rout. Herapid however onedthe lyaband ionandm discuss htoward adeadas tseat savacan.

Slater is a few hour in in fron aw him aga resaintl tof the ga rossed in azareeng ation wit a convers who was te ha friend to get the lling him nof his ov top butto ised ercoatra.

Permutations by groups of 9, 10, 11 and 12 letters

Ards midda one day tow r platform yon the rea saw a young of an S bus I eck was too man whosen o was weari long and wh ha plaited nga hat wit it cord round. Started toh suddenly he neighbourc arangue his the purpose laiming tha stoes every ly trod on hi got in or out time anyone. Pidly abando however he ra ssion and mad ned the discu acant seat ea dash for av.

Er I saw him aga a few hours lat he gare Saintl in in front oft edina convers azare engross iend who waste ation with afr tthe top button lling him toge at raised a bit nof his overco.

Permutations by groups of 1, 2, 3 and 4 words

Day one midday towards the on platform rear
an of bus S saw I young a whose man was neck
long too who and wearing was hat a a with
cord plaited it round. Started to suddenly he
neighbour claiming harangue his purposely
trod that he toes every on his got in time
anyone or out. Abandoned the discussion however he rapidly dash for a and made a vacant
seat.

I saw him again a few hours later gare Saint-
Lazare engrossed in front of the a friend who
was in a conversation with the top button of
telling him to get his overcoat raised somewhat.

Hellenisms

In a hyperomnibus full of petrolonauts in a chronia of metarush I was a martyr to this microrama; a more than icosimetric hypotype, with a petasus pericycled by a caloplegma and a eucylindrical macrotrachea, anathematized an ephemeral and anonymous outis who, he pseudologed, had been epitreading his bipods, but as soon as he euryscoped a coenotopia he peristrophed and catapelted himself on to it .

At a hysteretic chronia I aesthesised him in front of the siderodromous hagiolazaric stathma; peripating with a compsanthropos

134

who was symbouleuting him about the metaki-
netics of a sphincterous omphale.

Reactionary

Naturally the bus was pretty well full and the conductor was surly. You will find the cause of these things in the 8-hour day and the nationalisation schemes. And then the French lack organisation and a sense of their civic duties otherwise it wouldn't be necessary to distribute numbered tickets to keep some semblance of order among the people waiting to get on the bus—order is the word all right! That day there were at least ten of us waiting in the blazing sun, and when the bus did arrive there was only room for two, and I was the sixth. Luckily I said "On Government business" and showed a card with my photo and a tricolour band across it—that always impresses conductors—and I got on. Naturally I have nothing to do with the unspeakable republican government but all the same I wasn't going to miss an important business luncheon for a vulgar question of numbers. On the platform we were packed together like sardines. Such disgusting promiscuity always causes me acute suffering. The only possible compensation is the occasional charming contact with the quivering hindquarters of a dainty little midinette. Ah youth, youth! But one shouldn't let oneself get excited. That time I was surrounded entirely by men, one of whom was a sort of teddy boy whose neck was of inordinate length and who was wearing a felt hat with a kind of plait round it instead of a ribbon. They ought to send all creatures of that sort off to labour camps. To repair the war damage. That caused by the anglo-saxons, especially. In my day we were Young Royalists, not Rock 'n Rollers. At any rate this young object suddenly makes so bold as to start abusing an ex-service man, a real one, from the 1914 war. And he doesn't even answer back! When you see such things you realise that the Treaty of Versailles was madness. As for the lout, he threw himself on to

137

a vacant seat instead of leaving it to the mother of a family. What times we live in!

Anyway, I saw the pretentious young puppy again, two hours later, in front of the Cour de Rome. He was in the company of another jackanapes of the same kidney, who was giving him some advice about his get-up. The two of them were wandering aimlessly up and down, instead of going off to break the windows at the communist headquarters and burn a few books. Poor France!

aiku

Summer S long neck
plait hat toes abuse retreat
station button friend

ree verse

the bus
full
the heart
empty
the neck
long
the ribbon
plaited
the feet
flat
flat and flattened
the place
vacant

140

and the unexpected meeting near the station
    with its thousand extinguished lights
of that heart, of that neck, of that ribbon, of
    those feet,
of that vacant place,
and of that button.

eminine

Lot of clots! Today round about midday (goodness it was hot, just as well I'd put odorono under my arms otherwise my little cretonne summer dress that my little dress-maker who makes things specially cheaply for me made for me would have had it) near the Parc Monceau (it's nicer than the Luxembourg where I send my son, the idea of getting alopecia at his age) the bus came, it was full, but I made eyes at the conductor and got in. Naturally all the idiots who'd got numbered tickets made a fuss, but the bus had got going. With me in it. It couldn't have been fuller. I was terribly squashed, and not one of the men

142

who had a seat inside dreamed of offering it to me. Ill-mannered lot! There was a man beside me who was quite smart (it's the latest thing, a plait round a felt hat instead of a ribbon, I'm sure *Adam* must have written up this new fashion), unfortunately his neck was too long for my liking. Some of my friends claim that if one part of a man's body is bigger than the average (for instance a nose that's too big) it's a sign of marked capacities in another direction. But I don't believe a word of it. In any case, this gentlemanly creature seemed to have the permanent fidgets and I was wondering what he was waiting for and when he was going to say something to me or extend an exploratory hand. He must be shy, I was thinking. I wasn't so wrong at that. Because all of a sudden he started to pick on another man who looked horrible anyway and who was purposely treading on his toes. If I'd been that young man I'd have punched him on the nose but instead he quickly went and sat down the moment he saw a vacant seat and what's more it didn't occur to him for a single moment to offer it to me. The things that happen in the country of Gallantry!

A bit later, as I was passing the gare Saint-

Lazare (this time I had a seat) I caught sight of him arguing with a friend (quite a nice looking boy I must say) about the cut of his coat (extraordinary idea to wear an overcoat on such a hot day but it does make you look correctly dressed of course). I looked at him but the idiot didn't even recognise me.

*allicisms *

One zhour about meedee I pree the ohtobyusse and I vee a zhern omm with a daymoorzuray neck and a shappoh with a sorrt of plaited galorng. Suddenly this zhern omm durvya loofock and praytongs that an onnate moossyur is marshing on his pyaises. Then he jetéed himself on to a leebr plahss.

Two hours tarder I saw lur angcore; he was se balarding de lorngue ang larzhe in front of the gare Saint-Lazare. A dahndy was donning him some cornsayes à propos of a button.

* Replacing *Anglicismes*

rosthesis

Bone aday gabout mmidday, con dthe drear splatform jof va kbus, snot vfar ffrom Sparc Omonceau, Oi znoticed ta wyoung gman twhose gneck twas ztoo plong hand awho hwas sexhibiting ga shat kwith va splaited acord xinstead yof va cribbon cround pit. Xsuddenly che tstarted tto mharangue this nneighbour, vclaiming pthat she fpurposely strod lon this xtoes yevery ktime many spassengers fgot sin for tout. Showever hhe crapidly babandoned dthe kdiscussion cand ythrew phimself qupon na dvacant tseat.

Na ffew hhours slater Oi esaw rhim pagain fin

ifront kof uthe agare Esaint-Blazare dengrossed
bin sconversation qwith ga pfriend ewho owas
ggiving rhim tsome madvice zabout tan nover-
coat bbbbbbbbbbbbbbbbb bbbbbbbbbbbbbutton.

penthesis

Once dazy abogut mildday own thye repar platforum oaf ann S bugs I swaw a yoqung mean whorse necok wars toto lonig aind whoo wafs wetaring a hart wipth a planited chord instelad omf a ribobon rogund ist. Alol off a spudden hoe stairted tao haranogue hiss neighybour, claimping thast hue puruposely throd okn hims tomes evoery toime anny pascsengers grot inn oar oust. Howzever hoe rampidly abdandoned thee discussipon anod thorew himshelf upokn a vacrant sheat.

A flew houris lafter I spaw hirm agrain ian frognt orf thue garge Satint-Labzare enigrossed
148

ion converosation wirth a foriend woho wars
tellying hism two gert tyhe tolp bustton off hirs
overycoat ragised a littttttttttttttttttttttttttttle.

aragoge

Oner dayt abouth middayt ona thed reary plat-
forma off an 84 cm. bust If perceiveda ar
youngk manx whoser necko wash tool longr
anda whor wash wearingx ar hate withy an
plaitedm corda insteady oft ah ribbone roundr
itv. Suddenlyk her startedd top haranguer hist
neighboury, claimingk thath her purposelya
troda ona hisa toest everyl timeo anyx passen-
gerss goth inn orr outh. Howevery hem
rapidlyb abandonedo theo discussionm andy
threwm himselft uponx at vacantz seate.

Ak fewd hourse laterl If sawn himp againo ink
fronth oft them garej Sainte-Lazaret engrosseda

ina conversationa witha ay friendy whor wash tellingk himn top getj them topt buttonx off hiss overcoatl raiseddddddddddddddddddddddd.

arts of speech

ARTICLES : the, a, an.

SUBSTANTIVES : day, midday, platform, S, bus, Parc, Monceau, man, neck, hat, cord, ribbon, neighbour, toes, time, passenger, argument, seat, hours, front, gare, Saint, Lazare, conversation, friend, opening, overcoat, tailor, button, little.

ADJECTIVES : aforesaid, back, competent, encircled, engrossed, every, free, long, one, plaited, some.

VERBS : to notice, to wear, to start, to interpellate, to claim, to tread, to get, to abandon, to go, to throw, to see, to tell, to reduce, to get, to raise.

Pronouns : I, he, his, him, himself, who.

Adverbs : near, very, instead, suddenly, purposely, in, out, quickly, later, again.

Prepositions : about, on, of, with, by, down, in.

Conjunctions : that, or, but, and.

$\mathcal{M}$etathesis

Noe dya aobut dimday on teh rera platform of a sub, I toniced a nam whoes cenk saw oto glon nad whoes aht ahd a rost of strnig orund it. Dudsenly he cmailed hatt shi beighnour saw purspoely deatring on shi otes. Tub he adoived teh ueiss by wrothing shimelg on to a cavant teas.

Wot shour taler I was hmi anaig in tronf of teh rage Satin-Razale thiw an invididual woh saw gingiv hmi mose avdice atbou a nubbot.

Consequences *

A young man with a long neck and a hat with a plaited cord instead of a ribbon round it met another chap on an S bus. The young man said: "Sir, I have noticed that you have been taking a positive pleasure in stepping on my toes every time anyone gets on or off the bus." The other chap said: "Pah! B . . . . . ks!" and the consequence was that the young man went and sat down.

The same young man with the peculiar neck and the ridiculous hat met a pansified friend of his in the Cour de Rome. The young man said: "Hallo, how are you?" His pansified

155

friend said: "You really ought to get the top button of your overcoat raised," and the consequence was that a book was written and translated.

---

* Replacing *Par devant par derrière*

roper names

On the back Josephine of a full Leo, I noticed Theodulus, one day, with Charles-the-too-long, and Derby, surrounded by Plato and not by Rubens. All of a sudden Theodulus started an argument with Theodosius who was treading on Laurel and Hardy every time any Marco Polos got in or out. However, Theodulus rapidly abandoned Eris to park Fanny.

Two Huyghens later I saw Theodulus again in front of St. Lazarus in a great Cicero with Beau Brummel, who was telling him to go back to Austin Reed to get Jerry raised by a little Tom Thumb.

hyming slang *

I see a chap in the bus with a huge bushel and peck and a ridulous titfer on his loaf. He starts a bull and a cow with another chap and complains that he keeps treading on his plates with his daisy roots. Before the second chap can get his Oliver Twists at him he's run away.

Some bird-lime later I'm taking a butcher's out of the window of another bus and I see the same chap taking a ball o' chalk up and down with a china who has a Martin-le-Grand on the chap's overcoat.

* Replacing *Loucherbem*

Back slang *

Unway ayday aboutyay iddaymay onyay anyay essyay usbay Iyay oticednay ayay oungyay anmay ithway ayay onglay ecknay andyay ayay athay enyayircledcay ybay ayay ortsay ofyay ingstray inyayeadstay ofyay ayay ibbonray. Uddenlysay ehay artedstay anyay argumentyay ithway ishay eighbournay, ayay-usingkyay imhay ofyay eadingtray onyay ishay oestay. Ehay icklyquay abandonedyay ethay iscussionday andyay entway andyay ewthray imhayelfsay onyay ayay acantvay eatsay.

Ootay ourshay aterlay Iyay awsay imhay

againyay inyay ontfray ofyay ethhay aregay Aintsay-Azarelay enyayossedgray inyay on-vercayationsay ithway ayay iendfray owhay asway ellingtay imhay otay educeray ethay acespay atyay ethay openingyay ofyay ishay overyayoatcay ybay ettinggay ayay ompetent-cay ersonpay otay aiseray ethay optay utton-bay ofyay ethay overyayoatcay inyay estion-quay.

Antiphrasis

Midnight. It's raining. The buses go by nearly empty. On the bonnet of an AI near the Bastille, an old man whose head is sunk in his shoulders and who isn't wearing a hat thanks a lady sitting a long way away from him because she is stroking his hands. Then he goes to stand on the knees of a man who is still sitting down.

Two hours earlier, behind the gare de Lyon, this old man was stopping up his ears so as not to hear a tramp who was refusing to say that he should slightly lower the bottom button of his underpants.

Dog latin

Sol erat in regionem zenithi et calor atmospheri magnissima. Senatus populusque parisiensis sudebant. Omnibi passebant completi. In uno ex supradictis omnibibus qui S denominationem portebat, hominem quasi jungum, cum collo multo elongato et cum hatto by cordo plaitato cerclato vidi. Iste junior insultavit alterum hominem qui proximus erat: trodat, inquit, pedes meos post deliberationem animae tuae. Tunc sedem librum vidente, cucurrit ad it.

Sol duas horas in coelo habebat descended. Sancti Lazari stationem ferreamviam passente by, jungum supradictum cum altero ejusdem farinae qui arbiter elegantiarum erat et qui apropo uno ex buttonis capae junioris consilium donebat vidi.

ore or less

Won date bout mid Dane the plait former
finesse boss, I naughtiest aitch up with a nod
neck and a nodder rat—a bitterest ring a row
and it.   All over sodden he star tedder Cree
eight bee cause us odd was trading honest toast
on purpose. But then nurse eat bee came they
can't, Andy rushed often RQπ ditto band on
in the ark you meant.

Too ours lay terror sore him Infanta the Cars
and Ladder in gage din along conifer rents
Orly bout abut on.

164

pera English *

ACT I. *The Dandy, His Neighbour, The Conductor, Chorus of Passengers.*

1. *Opening Chorus of Passengers. "All Hail to Phoebus," etc.*

CHORUS OF PASSENGERS :
All hail to Phoebus meridian !
Long live the S quotidian !
But see ! that nullifidian
With hat of strange device !

His neck ! how long and skinny !
His voice ! how like a whinny !
As to a nearby Johnny
He speaks with prejudice.

165

2. *The Dandy. "Oh hear me, Gods!" Recit.*

DANDY:

Oh hear me, Gods! Gods, hear me! Why
should he on my toes tread?

I start, I quake, I tremble; I sweat and I
see red.

Ah! if to do it he continues—

But soft! he hears me!

NEIGHBOUR:

Oh say, what ails thee?

DANDY:

Sir, if thou continuest to tread on my trans-
ductor,

The Fates will surely constrain me to call,
Ah! the conductor.

NEIGHBOUR:

His words deep within my heart are sculptured.

3. *The Conductor. "My friends! See, see!"*
                    Recit. & Aria.

CONDUCTOR:

My friends! See, see! the traffic gathers all
around us! How shall we proceed? O
kindly traffic stream! that increaseth and
multiplieth so that total immobility is
reached and the weary passengers will
thus listen to my song—to thee I give

166

thanks.   I start, I quake, I tremble, the
sweat pours off my brow—but I will
sing it.

FEMALE PASSENGER :
Oh! I am fainting! (*faints*)

CONDUCTOR :
O sweet and friendly traffic stream,
This token of my high esteem
      Receive!
To thee and thy continued favour
Is due this modest semi-quaver—
      This breve!

How sweet to me thy diesel fumes,
Thy breath the air of night perfumes
      And day!
For when we cannot move along
Then listen those to my heartfelt song
      Who pay!

PASSENGERS :
Bravo Bravo Bravo Bis Encore Bravo.

CONDUCTOR :
Thank you, my friends, thank you.
   (*Repeats his Aria*)

PASSENGERS :
Bravo Bravo Bravo.

NEIGHBOUR (*to Dandy*) :
Sir—

167

PASSENGERS :
　　He has departed !
NEIGHBOUR :　Ah !

ACT II

4.　*Final Chorus of Passengers.　"Ah! once
　　again we see him.*
PASSENGERS :
　　Ah ! once again we see him
　　In front of Saint-Lazare,
　　Ah ! what a great coincidence,
　　'Tis he ! Oh how bizarre !
　　But see ! that friend who with him talks
　　Of buttons, goes too far,
　　Too far, ah ! too far,
　　But see ! that friend who with him talks
　　Of buttons, goes too far,
　　Of buttons, of buttons,
　　Of buttons, goes too far.

* Replacing *Italianismes*

or ze Frrensh

Wurn dayee abaout meeddayee Ahee got een-
too a büss ouich ouoz goeeng een ze deerekssion
off ze Porte Champerret. Eet ouoz fool, nearlee.
Ahee got een all ze sahme ahnd Ahee saw a
mahn een eet oo ahd a lorng neck ahnd a aht
ouiz a sorrt off playted streeng round eet. Zees
mahn got ahngree ouiz a shahp oo ouoz trreed-
ing ohn eez toes, ahnd zen ee ouent ahnd saht
daoun.
A beet lattère Ahee saw eem again een frronnt
off ze gare Saint-Lazare ouiz a dahndy oo ouoz
ahdveesing eem to move eez ohverrcowat
bouton a leetle beet ayère urp.

* Replacing *Poor lay Zanglay*

169

Spoonerisms

One May about didday, on the bear fatborm of a plus, I maw a san with a nery vong leck and whose cat was enhircled by a pliece of straited pling. Chuddenly this sap rarted a stow with a tan who was meading on his troes. Hen he thurried off to fret a geat which was see.

Two lours hater I haw gim asain in lont of the frare Gaint-Sazare, advistening to the lice of a lart asmec.

otanical

After nearly taking root under a heliotrope, I managed to graft myself on to a vernal speedwell where hips and haws were squashed indiscriminately and where there was an overpowering axillary scent. There I ran to earth a young blade or garden pansy whose stalk had run to seed and whose nut, cabbage or pumpkin was surmounted by a capsule encircled by snakeweed. This corny, creeping sucker, transpiring at the palms, nettled a common elder who started to tread his daisies and give him the edge of his bristly ox-tongue, so the sensitive plant stalked off and parked himself.

Two hours later, in fresh woods and pastures new, I saw this specimen again with another willowy young parasite who was shooting a line, recommending the sap to switch the top bulbous vegetable ivory element of his mantle blue to a more elevated apex—as an exercise in style.

Medical

After a short session of heliotherapy I was afraid I might get put in quarantine but I managed to climb without mishap into an ambulance full of stretcher cases. Amongst them I diagnosed a dyspeptic who was suffering from chronic gigantism with tracheal elongation and who was wearing a hat whose ribbon was deformed by rheumatism. This cretin suddenly worked himself up into a hysterical fit because a cacochymic was pounding his gomphous tylosis; then, having discharged his bile, he isolated himself to nurse his convulsions.

I saw him again later, he was standing outside a Lazaretto looking haggard and engaged in a consultation with a quack about a furuncle which was disfiguring his pectorals.

busive

After a stinking wait in the vile sun I finally got into a filthy bus where a bunch of bastards were squashed together. The most bastardly of these bastards was a pustulous creature with a ridiculously long windpipe who was sporting a grotesque hat with a cord instead of a ribbon. This pretentious puppy started to create because an old bastard was pounding his plates with senile fury, but he soon climbed down and made off in the direction of an empty seat that was still damp with the sweat of the buttocks of its previous occupant.

Two hours later, my unlucky day, I came

upon the same bastard holding forth with another bastard in front of that nauseating monument they call the gare Saint-Lazare. They were yammering about a button. Whether he has his furuncle raised or lowered, I said to myself, he'll still be just as lousy, the dirty bastard.

astronomical

After slowly roasting in the browned butter of the sun I finally managed to get into a pistachio bus which was crawling with customers as an overripe cheese crawls with maggots. Having paid my fare, I noticed among all these noodles a poor fish with a neck as long as a stick of celery and a loaf surmounted by a ridiculous donkey's dinner. This unsavoury character started to beef because a chap was pounding the joints of his cheeses to pulp. But when he found that he had bitten off more than he could chew, he quailed like a lily-livered dunghill-cock and bolted off to stew in his own juice.

I was digesting my lunch going back in the bus when I saw this half-baked individual in front of the buffet of the gare Saint-Lazare with a chap of his own kidney who was giving him the fruit of his experience on the subject of garnishing his coating, with particular reference to a cheese plate.

oological

In the dog days while I was in a bird cage at feeding time I noticed a young puppy with a neck like a giraffe who, like the toad, ugly and venomous, wore yet a precious beaver upon his head. This queer fish obviously had a bee in his bonnet and was quite bats, he started yak-yakking at a wolf in sheep's clothing claiming that he was treading on his dogs with his beetle-crushers. But the sucker got a flea in his ear; that foxed him, and quiet as a mouse he ran like a hare for a perch.

I saw him again later in front of the Zoo with a young buck who was telling him to bear in mind a certain drill about his fevvers.

179

utile

How can one describe the impression created by the contact of ten bodies squeezed together on the back platform of an S bus one day about noon near the rue de Lisbonne? How can one express the impression made by the sight of an individual with a neck so long as to be deformed and with a hat whose ribbon has been replaced, no one knows why, by a bit of string? How can one convey the impression given by a quarrel between a placid passenger unjustly accused of purposely treading on the toes of someone and that grotesque someone happening to be the individual described above? How can one translate the impression

180

provoked by the latter's flight, disguising his feeble cowardice by pretending to benefit by a seat?

Finally, how can one formulate the impression caused by the reappearance of this specimen in front of the gare Saint-Lazare two hours later accompanied by a well-dressed friend who was suggesting a sartorial amelioration to him?

M odern style

In a bus one day it so happened that I was a witness of the following as you might say tragi-comedy which revealing as it does the way our French cousins go on these days I thought I ought to put you in the picture. When the bus is full all the passengers fore-gather on the back platform, and one of them was a fancy-pants of the first water with a fantastic long neck and a hat with a plaited cord or what have you round it and a pansy sort of overcoat—the lot. All very pricey, no doubt, but definitely not my cup of tea. Well this chap, what he did, he started to go for the chap standing next to him, claimed he kept

182

treading on his toes if you please. Whether he was or wasn't I wouldn't know, to tell the truth I never saw, but if he was, well, fair enough, I mean to say, these sort of smart alecs there ought to be a law against them. Not that I'm so particularly choosy myself — I really couldn't care less. I reckoned he'd have his work cut out to cut any ice, and to be fair I must say I was right. What do you know, he just ran away. How yellow can you get?

Well, the thing is, two hours later I saw him again, he was with another chap who was giving him some technical know-how. He was telling him he ought to contact a tailor to move a button on that pansy overcoat of his, it was a must.

*P*robabilist

The contacts between inhabitants of a large town are so numerous that one can hardly be surprised if there occasionally occurs between them a certain amount of friction which generally speaking is of no consequence. It so happened that I was recently present at one of these unmannerly encounters which generally take place in the vehicles intended for the transport of passengers in the Parisian region in the rush hours. There is not in any case anything astonishing in the fact that I was a witness of this encounter because I frequently travel in this fashion. On the day in question the incident was of the lowest order, but my

184

attention was especially attracted by the physical aspect and the headgear of one of the protagonists of this miniature drama. This was a man who was still young, but whose neck was of a length which was probably above the average and whose hat-ribbon had been replaced by a plaited cord. Curiously enough I saw him again two hours later engaged in listening to some advice of a sartorial order which was being given to him by a friend in the company of whom he was walking up and down, rather nonchalantly I should have said.

There was not much likelihood now that a third encounter would take place, and the fact is that from that day to this I have never seen the young man again, in conformity with the established laws of probability.

ortrait

The styal is a very long-necked biped that frequents the buses of the S-line at about midday. It is particularly fond of the back platform where it can be found, wet behind the ears, its head covered by a crest which is surrounded by an excrescence of the thickness of a finger and bearing some resemblance to a piece of string. Of peevish disposition, it readily attacks its weaker brethren, but if it encounters a somewhat lively retort it takes flight into the interior of the vehicle where it hopes it will be forgotten.

It may also be seen, but much more rarely, in
186

the environs of the gare Saint-Lazare in the shedding season. It keeps its old skin to protect it against the cold in winter, but it is often torn to allow for the passage of the body; this kind of overcoat should fasten fairly high up by artificial means. The styal, incapable of discovering these for itself, goes off at that time to find another biped of a closely related species which gives it exercises to do,

Styalography is a branch of theoretic and deductive zoology which can be cultivated at any time of year.

athematical

In a rectangular parallepiped moving along a line representing an integral solution of the second-order differential equation:

$$y'' + PPTB(x)y' + S = 84$$

two homoids (of which only one, the homoid A, manifests a cylindrical element of length $L > N$ encircled by two sine waves of period π immediately below its crowning hemisphere) cannot suffer point contact at their lower extremities without proceeding upon divergent courses. The oscillation of two homoids tangentially to the above trajectory has as a consequence the small but significant displacement of all significantly small spheres tangential to a perpendicular of length $l < L$ described on the supra-median line of the homoid A's shirt-front.

est Indian *

In a bus with bags of people on, only room for two-three more, it have a fellar with a string instead of a ribbon round he hat, and this fellar look at another test with a loud tone in he eye and start to get on ignorant and make rab about this test treading on he toes. The test start to laugh kiff-kiff and the fellar get in one set of confusion, he looking poor-me-one and outing off fast for vacant seat.

Later I bounce him up, he coasting lime in the Cour de Rome, it have another test giving him ballad, he advicing him : "You best hads get that button moved."

* Replacing *Paysan*

190

nterjections

Psst! h'm! ah! oh! hem! ah! ha! hey! well!
oh! pooh! poof! ow! oo! ouch! hey! eh!
h'm! pffft!

Well! hey! pooh! oh! h'm! right!

recious

It was in the vicinity of a midday July. The sun had engraved itself with a fiery needle on the many-breasted horizon. The asphalt was quivering softly, exhaling that tender, tarry odour that gives the carcinomous ideas at once puerile and corrosive about the origin of their malady. A bus in green and white livery, emblazoned with an enigmatic S, came to gather from the neighbourhood of the Parc Monceau a small and favoured batch of postulant-passengers into the moist confines of sudiferous dissolution. On the back platform of this masterpiece of the contemporary French automobile industry, where itinerants were packed

192

together like sardines in a tin, an incorrigible rascal who was slowly advancing towards the commencement of his fourth decade and who was carrying between a neck of almost serpentine length and a hat encircled by a cordelet a head as insipid as it was leaden raised his voice to complain with an unfeigned bitterness which seemed to emanate from a glass of gentian-bitters, or from any other liquid of similar properties, of a phenomenon of the nature of a recurring blow or shock which in his opinion had its origin in a *hic et nunc* present co-user of the P.P.T.B. In order to give utterance to his lament he adopted the acid tones of a venerable vidame who gets his hindquarters pinched in a public privy and who strange to state does not at all approve of this compliment and is not at all that way inclined.

Later, when the sun had already descended by several degrees the monumental stairway of its celestial parade and when I was once more causing myself to be conveyed by another bus of the same line, I perceived the individual described above displacing himself in a peripatetic fashion in the Cour de Rome in the company of an individual *ejusdem farinae* who was giving him, in this locality dedicated to auto-

193

mobilistic circulation, sartorial advice which hung by the thread of a button.

Unexpected

They were sitting round a café table when Albert joined them. René, Robert, Adolphe, Georges and Théodore were there.
"How's everything?" asked Robert amicably.
"All right," said Albert.
He called the waiter.
"I'll have a picon," he said.
Adolphe turned towards him :
"Well, Albert, what's new?"
"Nothing much."
"Nice day," said Robert.
"Bit cold," said Adolphe.
"Oh I say, I saw something funny today," said Albert.

195

"It is warm though," said Robert.

"What?" asked René.

"In the bus, going to lunch," replied Albert.

"What bus?"

"The S."

"What did you see?" asked Robert.

"I had to wait for at least three before I could get on."

"Not surprising at that time of day," said Adolphe.

"Well, what did you see?" asked René.

"We were terribly squashed," said Albert.

"Good opportunity for pinching bottoms."

"Pooh," said Albert. "'That's got nothing to do with it."

"Go on, then."

"There was a queer sort of chap next to me."

"What was he like?" asked René.

"Tall, skinny, with a queer sort of neck."

"What was it like?" asked René.

"As if someone'd been having a tug of war with it."

"An elongation," said Georges.

"And his hat, now I come to think of it; a queer sort of hat."

"What was it like?" asked René.

"Didn't have a ribbon, but a plaited cord round it."

196

"Funny," said Robert.

"Then again," continued Albert, "he was the peevish type."

"How come?" asked René.

"He started to pick on the chap next to him."

"How come?" asked René.

"He said he was treading on his toes."

"On purpose?" asked Robert.

"On purpose," said Albert.

"And then what?"

"Then what? He simply went and sat down."

"Is that all?" asked René.

"No. Funny thing is, I saw him again two hours later."

"Where?" asked René.

"In front of the gare Saint-Lazare."

"What was he doing there?"

"I don't know," said Albert. "He was walking up and down with a pal who was calling his attention to the fact that the button of his overcoat was a bit too low."

"That is in fact the advice I was giving him," said Theodore.

Some New Directions Paperbooks

For complete listing request complete catalog from
New Directions, 80 Eighth Avenue, New York 10011   † Bilingual